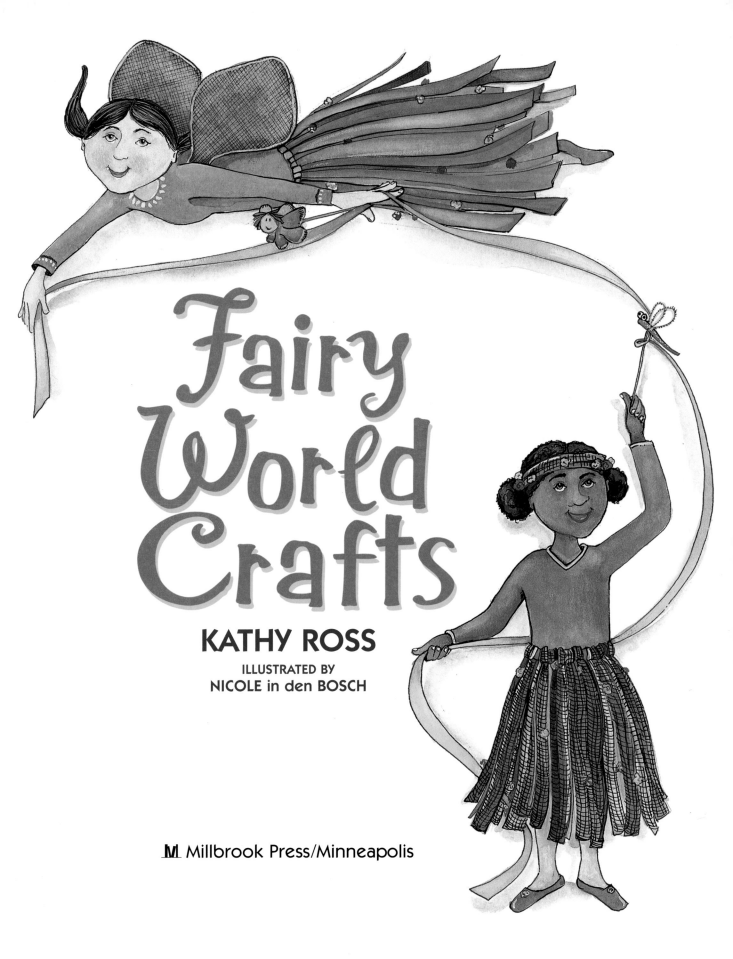

Fairy World Crafts

KATHY ROSS

ILLUSTRATED BY
NICOLE in den BOSCH

Ⱞ Millbrook Press/Minneapolis

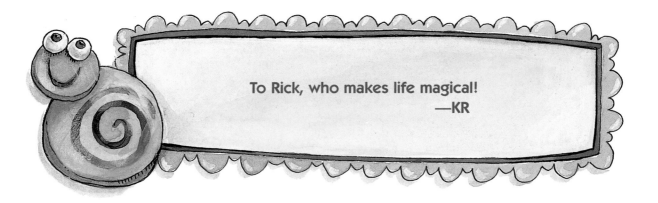

To Rick, who makes life magical!
—KR

Text copyright © 2008 by Kathy Ross
Illustrations © 2008 by Lerner Publishing Group, Inc.

Millbrook Press
A division of Lerner Publishing Group, Inc.
241 First Avenue North
Minneapolis, MN 55401 U.S.A.

Website address: www.lernerbooks.com

Library of Congress Cataloging-in-Publication Data

Ross, Kathy (Katharine Reynolds), 1948–
    Fairy World Crafts / by Kathy Ross ; illustrated by Nicole in den Bosch.
      p.   cm. — (Girl crafts)
    Includes bibliographical references and index.
    ISBN: 978–0–8225–7509–2 (lib. bdg. : alk. paper)
    1. Handicraft—Juvenile literature. 2. Fairies in art—Juvenile literature. I. Bosch, Nicole
in den. II. Title.
    TT157.R674 2008
    745.5—dc22   2006039581

Manufactured in the United States of America
1 2 3 4 5 6 – JR – 13 12 11 10 09 08

Contents

Fairy Skirt and Headpiece 4

Starry Wand 6

Fairy Outfit 8

Fairy Wings 10

Flower Fairy Wand 12

Fairy Necklace 14

Leaf Fairy Pin 16

Jingle Bell Fairy Fob 18

Fairy Magnet 20

Tooth Fairy Tooth Holder 22

Toadstools 25

Fairy in Flight 26

Snail Friend 29

Cupcake Fairy 30

Fairy Log House 32

Butterfly Wings Fairy 34

Leaf Table and Bed 36

Dragonfly Friend 38

Fairy Display 40

Fairy Flying Lessons 42

Doll Fairy Outfit 44

Fairy Garden Maze 46

Dress up like a fairy!

Fairy Skirt and Headpiece

Here is what you need:

discarded pair
small-size panty hose

green plastic wrap

artificial flowers

spools of thin
craft ribbon

scissors

ruler

Here is what you do to make the skirt:

1. Cut the waistband from the panty hose. This will be the waistband for your fairy skirt.

2. Unroll a strip of plastic wrap twice as long as you want the skirt to be. Scrunch up the plastic so it's a long strip. Fold the center of the plastic strip over the waistband.

3. Cut a piece of ribbon to the same length.

4. Tie it in a knot around the plastic strip, below the waistband, to secure the plastic to the band. Make sure the ribbon ends hang down evenly.

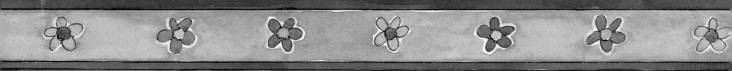

5. Cover the rest of the waistband with plastic strips and ribbons. The skirt's fullness will depend on how many plastic strips you use.

6. Tie artificial flowers to some of the hanging ribbons.

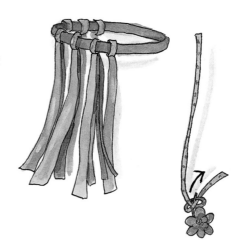

Here is what you do to make the headpiece:

1. Tear off a strip of plastic wrap long enough to wrap around your head once with some extra.

2. Wrap the plastic band around your head and remove it. Squeeze the strip together to create the headband.

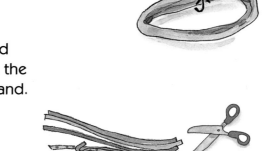

3. Cut six 4-foot (1.2-m) strips of craft ribbon. Tie them onto either side of the headband.

4. Tie some artificial flowers and leaves to the ribbons.

You might want to make your fairy costume with clear or a different-colored plastic wrap. If your skirt gets crushed, just pull apart the plastic strips to fluff it out again.

You'll need a magic wand!

Starry Wand

Here is what you need:

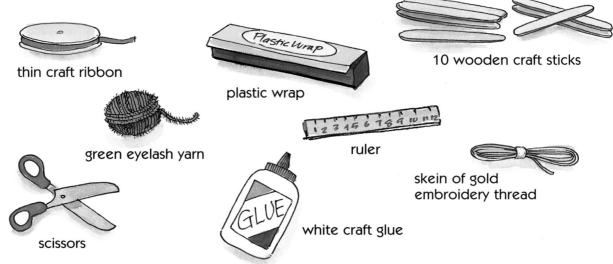

thin craft ribbon

plastic wrap

10 wooden craft sticks

green eyelash yarn

ruler

scissors

white craft glue

skein of gold embroidery thread

Here is what you do:

1. Place an 18-inch (46-cm) strip of plastic wrap on your work surface.

2. Place three craft sticks, end to end on the plastic wrap.

3. Glue an additional stick over each of the two points where the end-to-end sticks touch one another. This forms a sturdy handle.

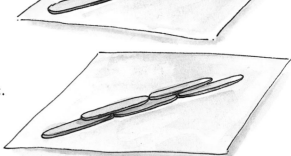

6

4. Shape the remaining five sticks into a five-pointed star. Glue the sticks together. Let dry.

5. Cut the gold thread into 1-inch (2.5-cm) pieces.

6. Cover one side of the star with glue. Sprinkle it with half of the gold thread. Let dry. Do the same thing on the other side of the star. Let dry.

7. Glue the star to the end of the handle.

8. Cover the handle with glue. Wrap it with the green eyelash yarn.

9. Cut two 2-foot (0.6-m) pieces of craft ribbon. Tie the ribbons to the wand.

Remember: don't use your wand to turn your brother into a frog!

Use bath scrubbies to make this fairy costume.

Fairy Outfit

Here is what you need:

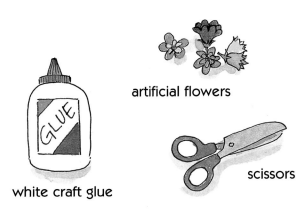

white craft glue

artificial flowers

scissors

3 to 5 plastic net bath scrubbies

ribbon

Here is what you do:

1. Cut the rope off each scrubby, creating a long net tube.

2. Cut each tube into strips twice as long as you want your fairy skirt to be.

3. Cut a piece of ribbon long enough to go around your waist and tie in a bow.

4. Tie the net strips along the ribbon so the ends hang down evenly to form the skirt. The skirt's fullness will depend on how many net strips you use.

5. Tuck artificial flower stems into the net skirt. Secure with glue.

GLUE

Make a headpiece to match the skirt by tying a long strip of net into a headband with the ends hanging down in back. Decorate the headpiece with ribbon and artificial flowers.

9

No fairy costume is complete without a set of wings!

Fairy Wings

Here is what you need:

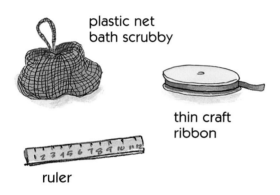

plastic net
bath scrubby

thin craft
ribbon

ruler

scissors

2 wire shirt
hangers

Here is what you do:

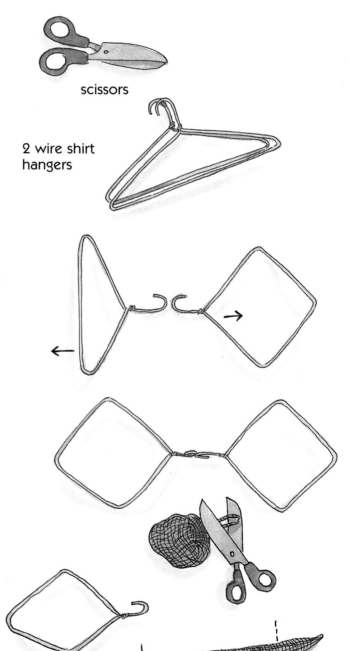

1. Pull on the bottom of each hanger to shape it like a wing.

2. Squeeze together the hooked part of each hanger wing.

3. Cut the rope off the scrubby, creating a long net tube.

4. Cut a piece of net tubing, more than twice as long as one of the wings.

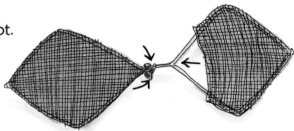

5. Knot one end of the net tube. Slip the net over the wing to cover it.

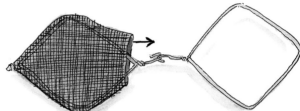

6. Knot the other end to close the net. Make sure there is excess net beyond the knot.

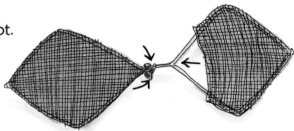

7. Cut another piece of net tubing. Cover the second wing in the same way.

8. Hold the hook ends of the two wings together. Wrap the excess net from both hangers around the hooks. Knot them to join the two wings together.

9. Cut two 4-foot (1.2-m) pieces of ribbon. Tie a ribbon around the base of each wing so that the two ends hang down on each side.

10. Tie the ribbon ends together around your chest under your arms.

Someone could also help you tie a set of ribbons loosely around the top of each arm so that you can slip the wings on and off.

11

This wand is perfect for a flower fairy.

Flower Fairy Wand

Here is what you need:

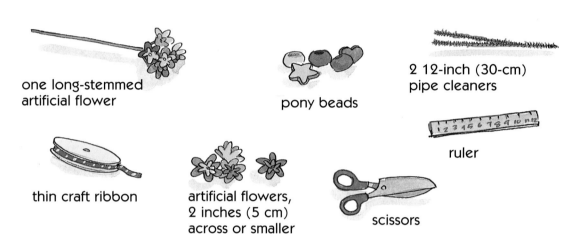

one long-stemmed
artificial flower

pony beads

2 12-inch (30-cm)
pipe cleaners

ruler

thin craft ribbon

artificial flowers,
2 inches (5 cm)
across or smaller

scissors

Here is what you do:

1. Hold the two pipe cleaners together.
Slide a pony bead onto one end.

2. Fold the two ends of the pipe cleaners
up around the bead on each side to secure it.

3. Separate the layers of petals from
several flowers by pulling out the stems
and plastic centers.

4. Thread the flower stem into the bead.
This is the wand handle.

5. Alternate threading beads and petals on the handle until you are about 3 inches (8 cm) from the end.

6. Curve over the pipe cleaner ends to secure the flowers and beads on the stem.

7. Separate the two pipe cleaners at the flower end. Thread pony beads on them.

8. When you reach each of the pipe cleaner ends, thread a flower petal and a pony bead to form a center for each flower.

9. Fold the end of each pipe cleaner over the pony bead to secure.

10. Cut two 2-foot (0.6-m) pieces of ribbon. Tie them around the wand below where the two ends of the pipe cleaners separate. Let the ribbons hang down.

11. Slide three pony beads on each ribbon. Knot the ribbon below the beads to secure them.

Wave your pretty wand, and make some magic!

Wear this necklace to keep your fairy friend with you everywhere you go!

Fairy Necklace

Here is what you need:

plastic container from gum ball machine

white
craft glue

fairy stickers

glitter

small artificial
flower head

thin craft ribbon

scissors

ruler

Here is what you do:

1. Turn the container on one side so that its clear top becomes the front of the necklace.

2. Open the container. Rub glue on the inside of the container.

3. Cut a 3-foot (0.9-m) piece of ribbon.

4. Press the ribbon ends into the glue to form the necklace hanger.

5. Press the small flower into the glue.

6. Shake the glitter over any remaining exposed glue.

7. Stick a fairy sticker on the flower.

8. Let the glue dry completely before snapping the top back on the container.

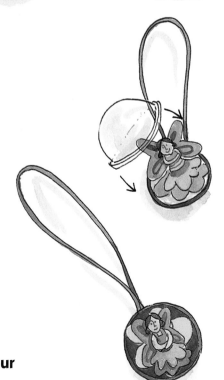

If you do not have any fairy stickers, draw your own little fairy on paper and use it instead.

This fairy will look wonderful on your coat.

Leaf Fairy Pin

Here is what you need:

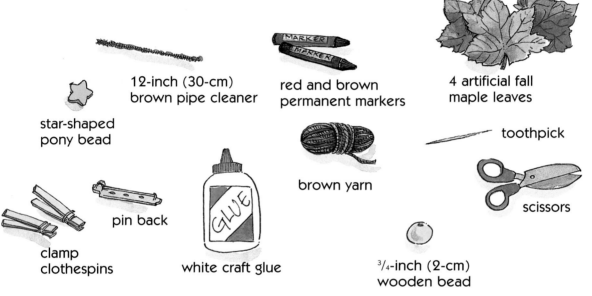

12-inch (30-cm) brown pipe cleaner

red and brown permanent markers

4 artificial fall maple leaves

star-shaped pony bead

toothpick

brown yarn

scissors

pin back

clamp clothespins

white craft glue

³/₄-inch (2-cm) wooden bead

Here is what you do:

1. Cut the pipe cleaner in half.

2. Fold one piece in half to form legs. Tip the ends out to form the feet.

3. Slide the wooden bead over the top fold for the head. Secure with glue.

4. Use the markers to draw a face on the wooden bead head.

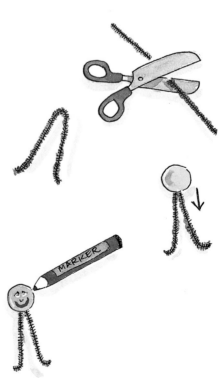

5. Cut yarn bits, and glue them to the head for hair. Make the hair as long as you want.

6. Wrap the second piece of pipe cleaner around the center of the first to form arms.

7. Glue a leaf over the front of the body for a dress.

8. Cut holes on each side of a second leaf. Slide the arms through the holes. Glue the second leaf in place over the first.

9. Glue a leaf sticking out from each side of the back of the fairy for the wings. Secure the leaves together with clothespins until the glue is dry.

10. Glue the star-shaped bead to one end of the toothpick for a wand. Cut the point off the other end.

11. Trim the arms if they seem too long. Wrap the end of one pipe cleaner arm around the wand. Secure with glue.

12. Glue a pin back to the back of the fairy.

If you don't have any craft leaves, cut leaves from felt or craft foam.

Hang a fairy from your book bag.

Jingle Bell Fairy Fob

Here is what you need:

paper clip

pipe cleaner

¾-inch (2-cm) wooden bead

2 large and 2 small artificial flowers

permanent markers

scissors

white craft glue

large jingle bell

ruler

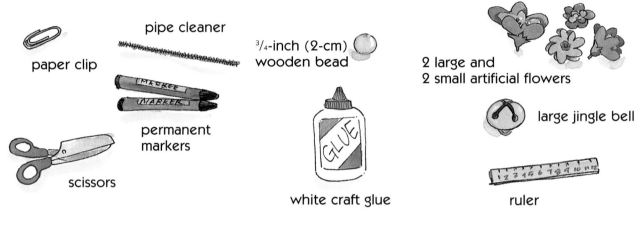

Here is what you do:

1. Cut a 4-inch (10-cm) piece of pipe cleaner.

2. Fold the piece of pipe cleaner in half.

3. Thread the jingle bell onto one end of the pipe cleaner. Slide the bell down to the fold.

4. Pull the plastic stems and centers from the flowers to separate the petal layers.

5. Slide two or more layers of large petals over both stems of the pipe cleaner to cover the jingle bell and form a dress.

6. Slide the bead over the two stems of the pipe cleaner above the flower dress. Use the markers to draw a face on the bead head.

7. Slide two layers of small flower petals over both stems for the hat. Secure with glue.

8. Wrap the two ends of the pipe cleaner together to form a hanger at the top.

9. Slide the paper clip on the hanger. You can use it to attach the fairy to a zipper tab.

This fairy would also look cute hanging from your jacket zipper.

Fly a fairy on your fridge!

Fairy Magnet

Here is what you need:

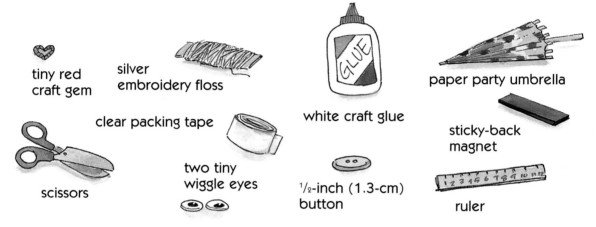

tiny red craft gem

silver embroidery floss

clear packing tape

scissors

two tiny wiggle eyes

white craft glue

½-inch (1.3-cm) button

paper party umbrella

sticky-back magnet

ruler

Here is what you do:

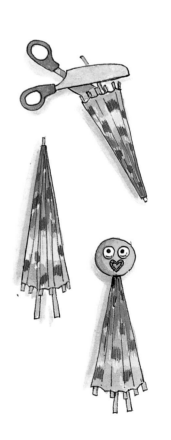

1. Cut off half the umbrella handle.

2. Glue the piece you cut inside the umbrella shaft next to the handle. These handle pieces are the fairy's two legs. The umbrella should be in the loosely closed position.

3. Glue the button to the umbrella tip for the head. Glue the wiggle eyes and the craft gem to the button to make a face.

4. Cut 2½-inch (6.4-cm) strands from the silver embroidery floss. Separate the strands. Glue them to the back of the button head to make hair.

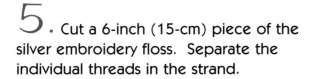

5. Cut a 6-inch (15-cm) piece of the silver embroidery floss. Separate the individual threads in the strand.

6. Cut two 6-inch (15-cm) pieces of packing tape. Set the strands on the sticky side of one piece of tape. Cover the strands with the second piece of tape.

7. Fold the tape pieces in half. Cut a single wing on the fold. When you open the fold, you have a set of wings.

8. Glue the center of the wings to the back of the fairy.

9. Press a strip of sticky-back magnet to the back of the fairy.

Make several fairy friends using different colored umbrellas and embroidery floss.

This fairy will hold your tooth for pick up by the tooth fairy.

Tooth Fairy Tooth Holder

Here is what you need:

small artificial flowers

small white pom-pom

yarn for hair

flip-flop shoe

eyelash yarn

white craft glue

clear plastic freezer bag

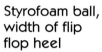
Styrofoam ball, width of flip flop heel

stretchy glove

2 large wiggle eyes

red pony bead

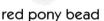
ruler

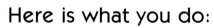
thin craft ribbon

scissors

Here is what you do:

1. Remove the strap from the flip-flop.

2. Cut a 3-foot (0.9-c) piece of ribbon. Wrap it around the flip-flop, back to front.

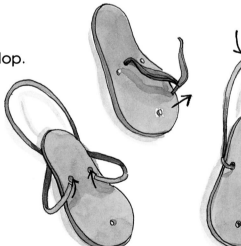

22

3. Thread the ribbon ends through the holes on each side, front to back, and pull tight. Tie the ends in a knot, forming the hanger.

4. Cut about one-third off the Styrofoam ball. Glue the larger piece to the heel for the fairy's head. The portion below the head will be the dress.

5. Press the pony bead into the Styrofoam. Glue the pom-pom above the pony bead mouth.

6. Glue on the wiggle eyes. Glue yarn pieces to the head for the hair.

7. Press the base of a flower into the hair and Styrofoam. Secure with glue.

8. Wrap the flip-flop dress with eyelash yarn. Secure with glue.

9. Glue a second flower in the bottom hole where the strap was removed.

(continued on next page)

10. Cut the cuff off the stretchy glove. Slide it over the flip-flop so that it is below the head, covering the two strap holes.

11. Cut two fingers from the glove for the arms and hands. Stuff them with scraps cut from the palm of the glove.

12. Glue the cut ends of each arm on each side of the fairy under the stretchy cuff.

13. Cut a tooth shape from the thumb of the glove. Glue the back to the hands of the fairy. This is the tooth holder.

14. Take the freezer bag and cut out two 8-inch (20-cm) long fairy wings.

15. Poke the wings through the two strap holes at the back of the fairy where you thread the ribbon through. Secure with glue.

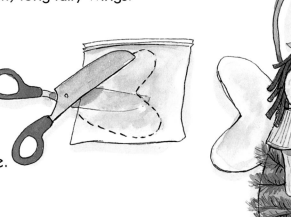

The tooth fairy can't miss finding your tooth with this pretty project!

Fairies like to sit on toadstools.

Toadstools

Here is what you need:

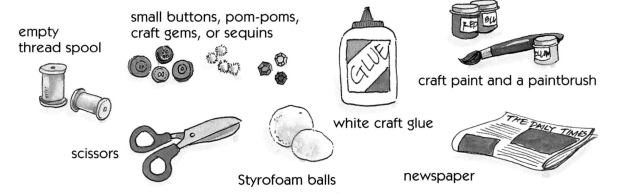

empty thread spool

small buttons, pom-poms, craft gems, or sequins

scissors

Styrofoam balls

white craft glue

craft paint and a paintbrush

newspaper

Here is what you do:

1. Cut off one-third of the Styrofoam ball.

2. Glue the larger piece to the top of the spool to make the toadstool.

3. Paint the toadstool.

4. Glue on small buttons, pom-poms, craft gems, or sequins for spots.

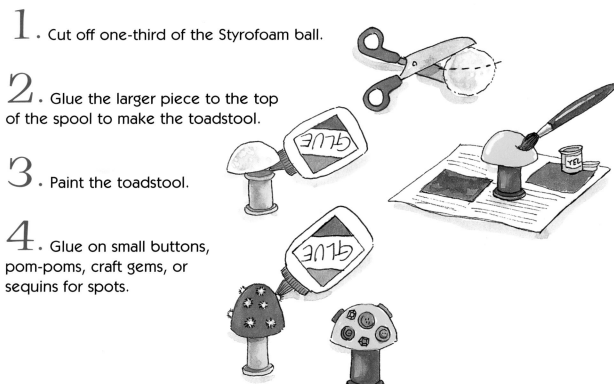

To sit a fairy on a toadstool, stick a 2-inch (5-cm) pipe cleaner into the top of the toadstool and slip the dress of the fairy over it.

Fly this fairy in a sunny window.

Fairy in Flight

Here is what you need:

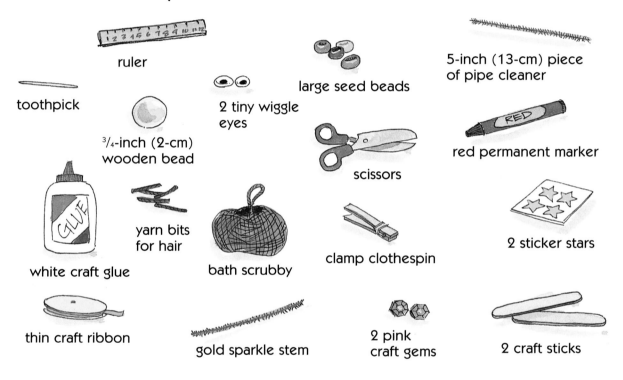

ruler

toothpick

2 tiny wiggle eyes

large seed beads

5-inch (13-cm) piece of pipe cleaner

¾-inch (2-cm) wooden bead

scissors

red permanent marker

white craft glue

yarn bits for hair

bath scrubby

clamp clothespin

2 sticker stars

thin craft ribbon

gold sparkle stem

2 pink craft gems

2 craft sticks

Here is what you do:

1. Fold the pipe cleaner in half. Glue the fold into the wooden bead.

2. Glue the craft sticks together in an X with the pipe cleaners between them. Make sure the bead head is above the center of the X. Secure with a clothespin. Let dry.

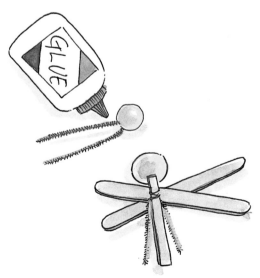

3. Cut the rope off the scrubby, creating a long net tube.

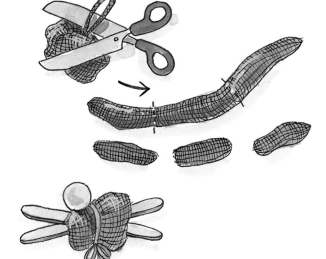

4. Cut pieces of net. Wrap them around the fairy to make the dress.

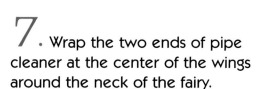

5. Secure the pieces by tying a piece of ribbon in a bow around the top portion of the dress.

6. Fold the sparkle stem in half. Shape the two ends into wings. Leave a 1½-inch (3.8-cm) piece hanging down from the two wings at the center.

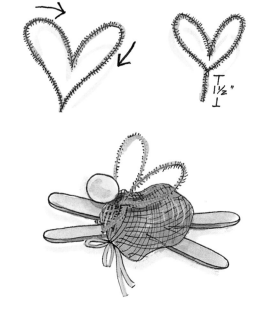

7. Wrap the two ends of pipe cleaner at the center of the wings around the neck of the fairy.

(continued on next page)

8. Draw a smile with the red marker. Glue the craft gems on each side for cheeks. Glue on the wiggle eyes.

9. Glue yarn bits to the head for hair.

10. Slide large seed beads onto the toothpick or color the toothpick with the marker.

11. Glue the two sticker stars together at the top of the toothpick wand.

12. Glue the wand in the fairy's hands.

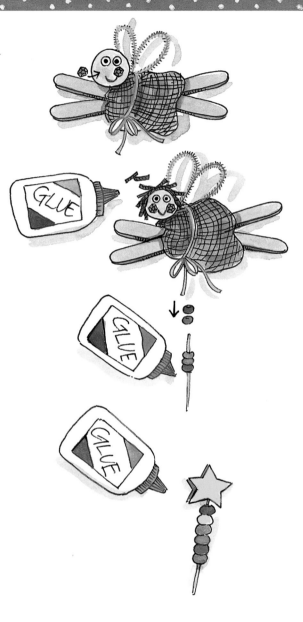

If you want to hang up the fairy, tie one end of a long piece of craft ribbon to the base of the wings. Tie a loop on the other end, and hang it from the window lock or a suction cup hanger on the window.

Make a pet for your fairies.

Snail Friend

Here is what you need:

2 large green glass plant gems

 **black permanent marker**

 white craft glue

2 small beads

2 white pony beads

2 small green glass plant gems

Here is what you do:

1. Glue the flat sides of the large gems together for the body.

2. Use the marker to draw a spiral shell pattern on both sides.

3. Glue the flat sides of the small gems together for the head. Glue the head to one side of the body.

4. Glue the pony beads to the top of the head for eyes. Glue a black bead in the center of each eye for pupils.

5. Use the marker to draw a smile.

This project works best if you allow the glue to dry between steps.

This fairy can be displayed by slipping the end of the wire into the toadstool project.

Cupcake Fairy

Here is what you need:

wooden bead

 scraps of brown eyelash yarn

 red seed bead

 2 paper cupcake wrappers

 2 tiny wiggle eyes

 1 foil cupcake wrapper

 white craft glue

 stapler

 wire or pipe cleaner

 scissors

 12-inch (30-cm) pipe cleaner

 ruler

Here is what you do:

1. Cut the 12-inch (30-cm) pipe cleaner in half. Fold one piece in half for the body for the fairy.

2. Glue the wooden bead over the fold.

3. Wrap the center of the second piece of pipe cleaner around the body to form the arms. Trim if needed.

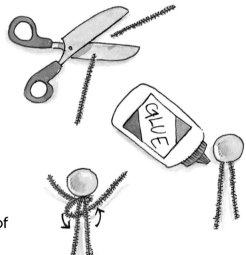

4. Stack the two paper wrappers together. Poke the pipe cleaner ends through the center. Slide the wrappers up to the neck. Secure with glue at the neck. Tip out the two pipe cleaner ends to form the feet.

5. Cut an 8-inch (20-cm) piece of wire or pipe cleaner for the base on which the fairy will fly. Slide the end of the wire up under the skirt and into the back of the bead head. Secure with glue in the bead head.

6. Fold the foil wrapper in half twice. Cut a pair of wings for the fairy with the fold as the center. Open the second fold so you have a set of wings. Staple the wings to the back of the fairy.

7. Glue the red seed bead to the head for a mouth. Glue on the wiggle eyes.

8. Glue bits of eyelash yarn to the head for hair.

You can also fly this fairy over the Fairy Log House.

Make a house for a fairy to live in.

Fairy Log House

Here is what you need:

ruler

4 wooden craft beads

brown paint and a paintbrush

craft moss

scissors

artificial flowers and leaves

white craft glue

large-size oatmeal box

black permanent marker

craft insects, butterflies

newspaper

2¹/₂-inch (6.4-cm) Styrofoam ball

Here is what you do:

1. Turn the box on its side to look like a log. Cut a 2-inch (5-cm) window in the center of the lid, and snap it back on the box.

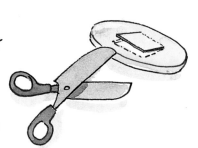

2. Cut a three-sided flap in the side of the box, 7 inches (18 cm) long and 5 inches (13 cm) wide. Carefully fold the flap up. The opening will be the door of the house.

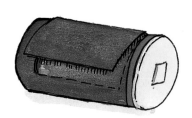

3. Cover the inside of the box and door with glue. Line it with craft moss, potpourri, artificial leaves, or similar material. Let the glue dry with the flap open so it will stay up.

4. Cut one-third off the Styrofoam ball. Glue the larger piece to the end opposite the window. You can insert wires here to fly fairies and insects.

5. Paint the outside of the box and the Styrofoam ball brown. Let dry.

6. Use the marker to draw bark lines. This makes the house look like a log.

7. Glue the four beads to the bottom of the house to keep it from rolling.

8. Glue artificial leaves, flowers, and craft insects to the outside of the house.

**One fairy can move into your little house,
while another can come for a visit!**

This little fairy will fit nicely in the Fairy Log House.

Butterfly Wings Fairy

Here is what you need:

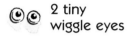 2 tiny wiggle eyes

wooden craft bead

 craft or appliqué butterfly

 2 tiny red or pink craft gems

 feather boa scrap

scissors

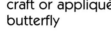 red and black permanent markers

 sparkle stem

 thin craft ribbons

 GLUE

 ruler

 embroidery floss, hair-colored

 white craft glue

Here is what you do:

1. Choose a bead that is in proportion with the butterfly wings you are using.

2. Glue one end of a 3-inch (8-cm) piece of feather boa into the bead hole. If the boa dress seems too long, trim it.

3. Use the marker to draw a smile and nose on the bead.

4. Glue on the wiggle eyes.

5. Glue a craft gem on each side of the mouth for cheeks.

6. Cut some embroidery floss into tiny bits. Glue them to the head for hair.

7. Cut a 3-inch (8-cm) piece of the sparkle stem.

8. Wrap the two ends of the sparkle stem around each other to make the fairy's headpiece.

9. Cut 5-inch (13-cm) pieces of ribbon to tie onto the headpiece. Let the ends hang down. Glue the headpiece to the top of the head.

10. Glue the fairy to the center of the butterfly wings.

If you think you might like to wear the fairy as a pin sometime, glue a pin back on the back.

Make furniture for a fairy.

Leaf Table and Bed

Here is what you need:

small empty thread spool

cardboard

4 3-inch (8-cm) artificial leaves

1/4-inch-wide (0.5-cm) stick from a tree or bush

brown craft paint and a paintbrush

white craft glue

petal from larger artificial flower

ruler

newspaper

clamp clothespins

scissors

tiny artificial flowers

Here is what you do to make the table:

1. Glue one leaf to the cardboard. Secure with clothespins until the glue is dry.

2. Cut out the cardboard-backed leaf.

3. Paint the cardboard side of the leaf and the edges brown. Paint the spool brown.

4. Glue the leaf to the top of the spool.

Here is what you do to make the bed:

1. Break off four 3-inch (8-cm) pieces of stick.

2. Cut a 3- by 4-inch (8- by 10-cm) piece of cardboard for the bed. Poke a hole in each of the four corners.

3. Slip a stick through each hole to make the legs and posts of the bed. Secure with glue.

4. Glue two leaves over the top of the bed to cover it. Glue a flower petal to one end for a pillow.

5. Set a leaf on top for a blanket.

6. Glue a tiny flower to the top of each bedpost.

You might want to glue tiny seashell plates or a wooden bead vase with flowers on the leaf table for the fairies.

Every fairy needs a dragonfly to ride.

Dragonfly Friend

Here is what you need:

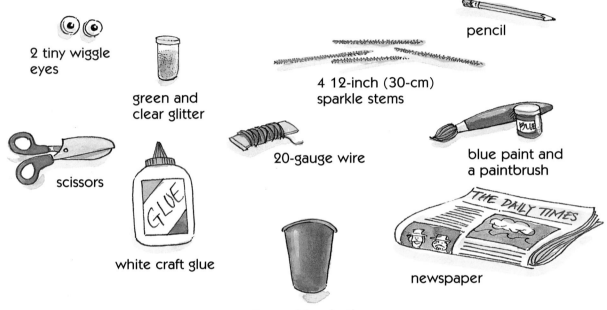

2 tiny wiggle eyes

green and clear glitter

4 12-inch (30-cm) sparkle stems

pencil

scissors

20-gauge wire

blue paint and a paintbrush

white craft glue

disposable plastic cup

newspaper

Here is what you do:

1. Sharpen the pencil down to a 6-inch (15.3-cm) length.

2. Break off the point by pressing it down on the newspaper.

3. Pour a small amount of blue paint into the cup. Add an equal amout of white glue. Stir with the paintbrush.

4. Paint the pencil with the paint and glue mixture.

5. Set the wet pencil on top of the cup and immediately sprinkle the pencil with green and clear glitter. Let dry.

6. Shape two of the sparkle stems into a dragonfly wing. Do the same with the other two.

7. Place the two wings on each side of the pencil. Twist the ends around the body. Secure with glue.

8. Glue the wiggle eyes to the eraser.

9. Cut an 8-inch (20-cm) piece of wire. Slip one end of the wire behind the wings. Fold the wire around itself to secure.

The wire allows the dragonfly to fly over the Toadstool or the Fairy Log House. If you would rather hang up the dragonfly, omit the wire and tie the end of a thin ribbon through the top of the wings.

Make a display box for your fairies.

Fairy Display

Here is what you need:

old picture frame or heavy cardboard

Potpourri
bag of potpourri with big pieces included

scrap of bark

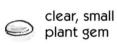
clear, small plant gem

Styrofoam ball

GLUE
white craft glue

pony bead

artificial flowers

box bottom with opening slightly smaller then the frame

craft store butterflies, insects (optional)

scissors

Here is what you do:

1. Cover the entire inside of the box with glue, then potpourri.

2. Glue the picture frame over the edge of the box. (You can also cut a frame from heavy cardboard and paint it.)

3. Glue some artificial flowers along the bottom, inside of the box. (You can also glue artificial flowers, leaves, or craft insects to outside of the frame.)

4. Glue the bark scrap inside the box on one side to look like a tree stump.

5. Glue the edge of the plant gem to the pony bead. Glue this gazing ball on top of the bark stump.

6. Cut the Styrofoam ball in half. Glue one-half on the back of the box.

7. Tuck some craft store insects into your display if you wish.

You can use this display to store your fairies or snails when they are not being used. You can also fly the Cupcake Fairy or the Dragonfly Friend by inserting them into the foam on the back of the display.

Help this fairy learn to fly!

Fairy Flying Lessons

Here is what you need:

scissors

permanent markers

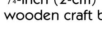

³/₄-inch (2-cm)
wooden craft bead

flexible straw

yarn bits for hair

cotton swab

3-inch (8-cm)
artificial flower

white craft glue

Here is what you do:

1. Cut the tip off one end
of the cotton swab.

2. Glue the craft bead to the cut
end of the swab for the head.

3. Use a marker to draw a line down
the center of the remaining cotton tip
to look like two feet on tiptoes.

4. Pull out the flower's stem and plastic center. Separate the petal layers.

5. Slide one layer over the cotton swab. Secure with glue under the bead head. This is the fairy's dress.

6. Cut two petals from another layer of the flower. Glue the two petals to the back of the fairy to look like wings.

7. Use the marker to draw a face on the bead head.

8. Glue yarn bits to the top of the head for hair. Let dry.

To "fly" the fairy, slip the cotton swab feet down into the bendable end of the straw. Aim where you want the fairy to go, and blow hard on the opposite end of the straw. How far can you fly your fairy?

Dress your doll like a fairy!

Doll Fairy Outfit

Here is what you need:

eyelash yarn

artificial flowers
and leaves

pipe cleaner

variety of ribbons

old sock with cuff
to fit over your doll

scissors

doll

Here is what you do:

1. Cut the cuff off the sock to a short tube dress length. Slide it onto your doll to make a bodysuit. The size of the sock needed will depend on the size of doll.

2. To make the waistband, cut a piece of ribbon long enough to go around the doll's waist and to tie in a bow.

3. Cut a piece of ribbon the distance between the waist and ankle of your doll.

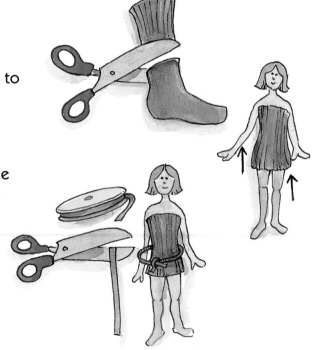

4. Cut more pieces of ribbon and eyelash yarn the same length.

5. Tie the pieces of ribbon and eyelash yarn around the waistband to form the skirt. Leave the two ends free to tie the bow.

6. Cut two leaves from the artificial flowers. Tuck the ends into the bodysuit cuff in back to form wings.

7. Cut a piece of pipe cleaner to make the doll's crown.

8. Thread the plastic centers from small flowers onto the crown.

9. Wrap the two ends of the crown together to secure it in a circle.

10. Cut six long ribbons. Tie them onto the crown. Let the ends hang down.

**Now you and your doll can both dress like fairies.
Fly her out to the garden to find some fairy friends!**

You can use this project as a skill game or as a setting for your fairy play.

Fairy Garden Maze

Here is what you need:

artificial leaves
and flowers

pencil

fairy stickers (or draw
your own fairies)

bag of potpourri

white craft glue

carton or large box
bottom (length and
width at least 16 inches)

ruler

small wooden
bead

scissors

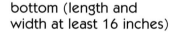
small stones
and pebbles

permanent
markers

Here is what you do:

1. Cut the sides of the box down to 3 inches (8 cm) high.

2. Use the markers to draw a stone wall or wooden fence with a gate.

3. Draw a winding path from one corner to the opposite corner. Add paths off it that dead-end. Erase the pencil lines where you have added dead-ends.

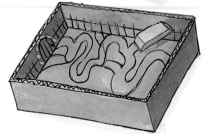

4. Cover the area between the paths with glue. Sprinkle with potpourri. Push the potpourri into the glue.

5. Before the glue has dried, make sure the bead can roll freely through the maze. If needed, widen the paths.

6. Glue small pebbles, artificial leaves, and flowers around the sides of the garden and among the potpourri.

7. Use the markers to write "Bug's House" on a stone. Glue it at the beginning of the maze.

8. Place a fairy sticker or picture at the end of the maze.

9. Use the marker to draw a bug face on the bead.

To play with the maze, roll the bug from the bug house through the garden maze to find the fairy. Tip the box in the direction you want the bug to go.

47

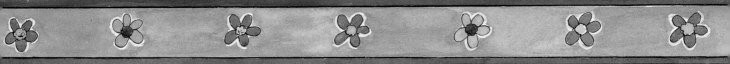

About the Author

With more than one million copies of her books in print, Kathy Ross has written over fifty titles and her name has become synonymous with "top quality craft books." Following twenty five years of developing nursery school programs and guiding young children through craft projects, Ross has authored many successful series, including *Crafts for Kids Who Are Learning about...*, *Girl Crafts*, and *All New Holiday Crafts for Kids*.